For my brave girls.
—K.A.

To my family.
—É.C.

The Book Dragon

by KELL ANDREWS · illustrated by ÉVA CHATELAIN

STERLING CHILDREN'S BOOKS
New York

**R**EADING WAS TIRESOME FOR ROSEHILDA. IN FACT, READING WAS TIRESOME FOR ALL THE CHILDREN IN LESSER SCRUMP.

Sometimes the schoolmaster, Mr. Percival, taught them letters by scrawling on bark with a stump of charcoal.

Sometimes he scribbled words on slate with a crumbly rock.

Every third Monday, he scraped a whole sentence in the dust of the schoolyard.

ONE DAY Rosehilda said, "Mr. Percival, reading would be more fun if the letters and words were written as **stories**. We could use paper and ink, then attach the papers together."

The children gasped. Mr. Percival
sent Rosehilda home with a stern note
scratched onto a leaf.

"What was wrong with what I said?"
Rosehilda asked her grandfather. "Why
can't we write on paper?"

"Because of the
Book Dragon," her
grandfather said.

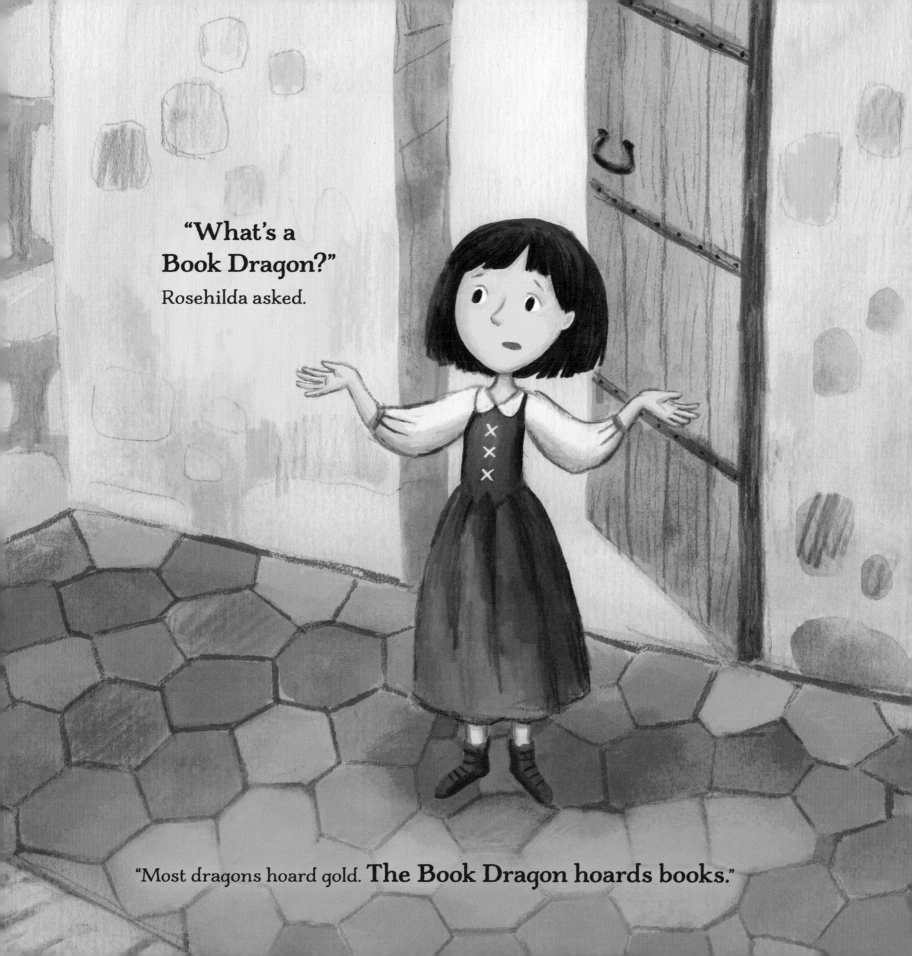

"What's a
Book Dragon?"
Rosehilda asked.

"Most dragons hoard gold. **The Book Dragon hoards books.**"

"What's a **book?**" Rosehilda asked.
"It's letters and words written on papers that
are attached together," her grandfather said.

Rosehilda knew it!

"The Book Dragon lives in a deep cave on Scrump Mountain, nesting on a pile of books nearly as tall as the mountain itself," her grandfather explained. "If any villager brings a book into Lesser Scrump, the Book Dragon snatches it away that night."

"**Mr. Percival, we need books,**" Rosehilda said the next day. "I'm not afraid of the Book Dragon, even if she snatches them away."

"You may not be afraid, but think of the rest of us," Mr. Percival said. "After the Book Dragon snatches a book, she comes back the next night, knocking on locked windows and terrorizing the entire village."

He sent Rosehilda home for a whole week with a stern note carved into an old candle stub.

ON THE WALK BACK Rosehilda met a peddler.

"Buy my wares, dearie?" she said.

Rosehilda noticed a square red object stamped in gold among the jumble in the cart. She knew just what it was.

"How much for the book?" she asked.

"What do you have?" asked the peddler.

"Just an old candle stub," Rosehilda said.

"Sold!" said the peddler, knowing the Book Dragon would snatch any book in Lesser Scrump by morning.

WHEN ROSEHILDA GOT HOME, she read a whole story, all about a brave knight who challenged a dragon and won the golden hoard. For the first time, reading wasn't tiresome. It was amazing!

When her grandfather saw her reading, he shook his head.

"I'm not afraid of the Book Dragon," Rosehilda said. She read until it was so dark she wished she had that candle stub. She laid the book by her bed and slept.

BY MORNING THE BOOK WAS GONE.

"The Book Dragon snatched it," her grandfather said. "We'll have to lock our windows tonight."

Now the Book Dragon would terrorize the village and it would be Rosehilda's fault. She couldn't let that happen! She vowed to challenge the dragon and win her book back.

When her grandfather left for work,
Rosehilda climbed the narrow path up
Scrump Mountain.

When she reached the dark cave at the top,
she reminded herself that she wasn't afraid,
although she wished again for that candle stub.

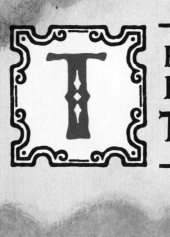

THERE, ON AN IMMENSE PILE OF BOOKS, PERCHED **THE BOOK DRAGON.**

She looked **very large** and **extremely pointy.**
Most of all, she looked **surprised.**

"Give me back my book!" Rosehilda demanded.
"You snatched it from my room last night."

"I beg your pardon," said the Book Dragon. "I can't help myself.
I love books so much! I'm too large to live in the village, so books are
all the company I have."

"That's no excuse for
stealing and terrorizing
the village!" Rosehilda said.

"I only want to **borrow** books," the Book Dragon said. "But when I try to return them, the windows are locked. Everyone shrieks when I knock."

Rosehilda understood why. The dragon **was** extremely pointy.

"Since you came all this way, I'll give your book back now," the Book Dragon said.

The hoard was heaped with books in every color and size. Many were red, stamped with gold. Rosehilda didn't know which was hers.

Rosehilda and the Book Dragon searched. They lined up the books in rows, sorted by subject and author. At the end of the day, they hardly made a dent in the hoard. Rosehilda hadn't found her book.

"You can borrow a different one," the Book Dragon said.

"I'll bring it back tomorrow,"
Rosehilda said.
    She borrowed a green book
and read until dark.

THE NEXT DAY Rosehilda and the Book Dragon sorted and searched.

They didn't find Rosehilda's book, so she borrowed a blue one.

BY THE END OF THE WEEK,
nearly all the books stood in neat rows.
The very last book was red, stamped
with gold.

"**My book!**" said Rosehilda.
"Now I won't need to come back."

The Book Dragon looked less
pointy than usual.

"You could borrow another book,"
the Book Dragon said. "And come back
tomorrow."

"I have an
even better idea,"
Rosehilda said.

THE NEXT DAY, just as Mr. Percival was scraping a letter on the dirty window, a large and pointy shape appeared outside.

The children gasped. Mr. Percival shrieked.

Rosehilda explained, "This is my friend, the Book Dragon. She brought our books back. She never meant to keep them." "After all," said the Book Dragon, "books are for reading, not hoarding."

The villagers agreed.

FROM THAT DAY FORWARD, they let the
Book Dragon lend the books from the library in
Scrump Mountain. Everyone in Lesser Scrump read as
much as they wanted without having to worry about a
dragon snatching books in the middle of the night.

Official
Village Library
of
Lesser Scrump

STERLING CHILDREN'S BOOKS
New York

An Imprint of Sterling Publishing Co., Inc.
1166 Avenue of the Americas
New York, NY 10036

STERLING CHILDREN'S BOOKS and the distinctive Sterling Children's Books logo
are registered trademarks of Sterling Publishing Co., Inc.

Text © 2018 Kell Andrews
Cover, jacket, and interior illustrations © 2018 Éva Chatelain

ISBN 978-1-4549-2685-6

Distributed in Canada by Sterling Publishing Co., Inc.
c/o Canadian Manda Group, 664 Annette Street
Toronto, Ontario M6S 2C8, Canada
Distributed in the United Kingdom by GMC Distribution Services
Castle Place, 166 High Street, Lewes, East Sussex BN7 1XU, England
Distributed in Australia by NewSouth Books
45 Beach Street, Coogee, NSW 2034, Australia

For information about custom editions, special sales, and premium and corporate purchases,
please contact Sterling Special Sales at 800-805-5489 or specialsales@sterlingpublishing.com.

Manufactured in China

Lot #:
2 4 6 8 10 9 7 5 3 1
07/18

sterlingpublishing.com

The artwork for this work was created using watercolor, colored pencils, and Adobe Photoshop.
Jacket and interior design by Ryan Thomann.